Super Puppies

Moose and Violet Knock Things Down

by Corey Powell
illustrated by Kristen Humphrey

Penguin Workshop

PENGUIN WORKSHOP
An imprint of Penguin Random House LLC
1745 Broadway, New York, New York 10019

First published in the United States of America by Penguin Workshop,
an imprint of Penguin Random House LLC, 2025

Text copyright © 2025 by Corey Powell
Illustrations copyright © 2025 by Kristen Humphrey
Cover illustration copyright © 2025 by arn0

Penguin Random House values and supports copyright. Copyright fuels creativity, encourages diverse voices, promotes free speech, and creates a vibrant culture. Thank you for buying an authorized edition of this book and for complying with copyright laws by not reproducing, scanning, or distributing any part of it in any form without permission. You are supporting writers and allowing Penguin Random House to continue to publish books for every reader. Please note that no part of this book may be used or reproduced in any manner for the purpose of training artificial intelligence technologies or systems.

PENGUIN is a registered trademark and PENGUIN WORKSHOP is a trademark of Penguin Books Ltd, and the W colophon is a registered trademark of Penguin Random House LLC.

Visit us online at penguinrandomhouse.com.

Library of Congress Cataloging-in-Publication Data is available.

Printed in the United States of America

ISBN 9780593750384

1st Printing

LSCC

Design by Taylor Abatiell and Aya Ghanameh

This book is a work of fiction. Any references to historical events, real people, or real places are used fictitiously. Other names, characters, places, and events are products of the author's imagination, and any resemblance to actual events or places or persons, living or dead, is entirely coincidental.

CHAPTER ONE

Pee Feet

Moose was the biggest puppy in the litter, which was why he usually ended up at the bottom of the pile. That morning was no different. He woke up to find Rocky's butt in his face, Sparkle's body draped around his neck, and Tobey using his hind legs as a pillow. But because he wasn't the kind of dog who thought much about things before he did them, Moose simply rolled to his feet and shook himself off like he was covered in water instead of siblings. Rocky slid across the floor with a yelp. Sparkle flew backward into a water dish, and Tobey rolled to the other end of the room. They turned furiously on Moose. No puppy liked to be woken up this way, especially super ones.

Rocky glowered at his brother. "Not okay, Moose!" He lowered his ears and thundered across the room. The top of his head butted harmlessly into Moose's side. They slid across the floor and crashed into the wall. The wall stopped

Moose, but Rocky went straight through it, briefly disappearing into the next room because his power was the go-through-solid-objects kind.

Sparkle stepped out of the water dish and shook herself off. She was soaked and wanted Moose to know just how much she DID NOT appreciate it. She flew at him, slamming into his neck with a wet thump. "I'm so totally telling! No bones for you tonight."

"I said I was sorry!" Moose claimed. But Sparkle knew this wasn't true, because Moose *never* remembered to apologize. She backed up and flew at him again because her power was the fly-through-the-air kind.

Tobey watched this exchange, waiting for her moment to exact revenge. She disappeared and then reappeared close enough to Moose to playfully nip his leg. It didn't hurt, but Moose still howled dramatically. "Big baby!" Tobey said as she disappeared again because her power was the disappear-and-reappear kind.

As Moose's siblings circled him, he didn't feel the least bit sorry. He was, in fact, joyful because there was nothing he loved more than a good game of chase. "I'm so gonna get you!" he said. The others wagged their tails and took off. Moose followed. He tried to chase Rocky under a table but forgot to duck.

He smashed through it, leaving nothing but splinters behind. "Oops!" he said as he spun around and wagged his tail right through a bookshelf because his power was the superstrong kind. As the books cascaded to the floor, Moose tucked his tail between his legs.

"Ooooh, you're in trouble!" Sparkle taunted. "Mom and Dad and the bigs aren't gonna like the mess you made."

Moose lowered his head and put his ears back. She was right. When there was a mess, he was almost always the one who made it. Tobey appeared out of thin air by his side and gently licked his ear. "Just remember to say you're sorry this time." They stared at the door, waiting for one of their parents or some of the other dogs in their pack to appear. They didn't. This was very strange, and Moose would've asked a lot of questions if he hadn't suddenly detected something in the air.

He smelled Shadow before he saw her. "Cat!" Moose yelled, right before their superpower instructor appeared on top of the recently destroyed bookshelf. The gray cat wrapped her tail around her body and observed the mess, silently taking in every detail before letting her eyes rest on Moose.

"I see," she said, without bothering to finish the thought, but Moose knew what she meant. He was almost always the one who couldn't control his power.

Sparkle still wanted payback for that dip in the water bowl. "Where is everyone . . . 'cause Moose is in big, big trouble!" When no one responded, she added, "At least, he should be."

Shadow blinked in that way-too-long way cats do and then continued, "I don't know where the rest of the pack is. They're gone. You're the only ones left."

Moose instantly felt warmth pooling around his feet. "Moose had an accident! He has pee feet!" Sparkle shrieked as she flew to the back of a couch to get away.

Tobey often used too many words

for a simple thought. "Remember how we're supposed to go outside for that? You gotta follow your nose, find the right spot, and then you can have your accident . . . except then it's not an accident, then it's what you're supposed to do. Are you sure you don't remember that?!"

Moose nodded as though his accident was something he could control any better than his superstrength. The idea of being without his parents or the rest of the big dogs was the biggest, scariest thought he'd ever had, and his bladder wanted to make sure everyone else knew it, too.

"What's happening, Shadow?" Rocky asked in his serious, trying-to-sound-like-a-big-dog voice, but Moose could tell his brother was afraid. They all were. Fear comes with the territory when you're special . . . and they were very, *very* special.

Moose, Sparkle, Rocky, and Tobey were the newest litter of puppies in a

superpack of dogs whose sole purpose was to keep the people on Earth safe. Shadow said, "It's time for you to meet your first humans."

Moose knew he should still be afraid, but the thought of meeting a human, any human, just made him so happy. His tail had a mind of its own. It began to move like a windshield wiper across the floor, flinging puppy pee across the room. The others scattered furiously and barked, "MOOOOSE!!"

Shadow squeezed her eyes shut like she might never open them again and waited. She waited until Moose sat on his tail and the others found dry spots where they could refocus on what she had to say. "Like I said. The rest of the pack has disappeared. I believe they're in the human world, and you need to find them."

The dogs looked at each other, wordlessly asking, *For real?!*

Shadow continued, "One of them left this behind." She used her paw to pull a bright, sparkly, obviously magic ball out of thin air. "I've seen this kind of magic before . . . This ball is one piece of a lock. When we get all of the pieces together, we will, hopefully, unlock whatever it is that's keeping the rest of the pack from coming back home."

Moose swallowed hard and asked, "And we're the ones who're supposed to find the balls?"

Instead of answering, Shadow flicked her tail, and the room filled with sparkles and colors. The puppies all felt it. This magic was powerful, stronger than what they were used to, and then they saw why. Four portals to the human world opened, one in front of each dog's nose. Moose saw wonderful things on the other side of his: humans walking, humans on bikes, humans playing Frisbee . . . and he didn't hesitate. He bounded through his portal, ready to leave the magic puppy world behind and finally meet some of those amazing humans.

CHAPTER TWO

The Fountain

Violet strolled through the park. It was a beautiful day, but she wasn't seeing any of it. She was looking at her favorite thing in all the world: her to-do list. Violet was the kind of girl who didn't like to leave things to chance. She always needed a plan, even if that plan was to walk through the park and look at her list, which was what she was doing when she heard the first scream. "There's a puppy in the fountain!" someone yelled.

Violet looked up to see an enormous wet puppy standing in the middle of the fountain. It was way too big to be in any kind of danger, and she wondered why this concerned group of citizens wanted to save it. The puppy didn't understand it, either. It charged its rescuers, joyfully smashing through the side of the fountain on its way. This created a small tsunami that swept the people off their feet and washed them across the pavement and into the grass. Violet watched as these citizens suddenly became less concerned about saving the puppy and more concerned about who was going to save *them* from the puppy.

    Violet forgot all about her list as everyone scrambled to their feet. She heard someone ask what was happening, but no one answered. They were too busy gaping at the puppy, which had just barreled through a park bench as though it wasn't made of metal and wood. And that was the end of the questions. The only things Violet heard were a few shrieks and the pounding of feet as everyone tried to get away. The people ran as fast as they could out of that park, and the puppy followed. It bounced left, right, back, and forth. It tried to chase everyone at once but ended up going nowhere. With a frustrated whimper, the puppy flopped to the ground and stared longingly after them.

Violet was suddenly aware that she and the puppy were the only two left in the park. She looked at her list and crossed out "take a walk in the park 'cause Daddy said I need to do something besides make lists" and replaced it with "escape from the Godzilla puppy." She took a step backward and then reconsidered. She crossed that out and wrote "meet Godzilla puppy and try not to die." She understood that this might be overly dramatic, but it was a *really* big puppy.

Violet took a brave step in the puppy's direction. It heard her and spun around with its paws down and butt in the air. It wagged its tail, and Violet thought this was a good start. She wasn't sure what the rules were for meeting a Godzilla puppy, but assumed a happy puppy was less likely to squash her . . . and then it wagged its tail right through the base of a streetlamp. As the lamppost toppled, Violet instantly regretted that she didn't go with her first plan and sneak away.

The puppy bounded over to sniff the fallen post, and Violet used this distraction to pivot and run toward the street. She lifted her knees and pumped her arms. It was the fastest she could run, but it wasn't nearly as fast as the puppy. She could feel it coming up behind her, getting closer with each thunderous step. She heard the snap of a small tree, the crash of an abandoned snow cone cart being overturned, and then a delighted "I'm so gonna get you!"

This voice from nowhere was such a surprise that Violet couldn't resist seeing where it came from. She whirled around just in time to see the puppy coming fast and hard in her direction. They both screamed, "AHHHHHHHH!" The puppy sat down but still couldn't stop. The momentum caused it to slide across the grass. They were on a collision course until the puppy pushed its front paws into the ground like a furry snowplow. Mounds of soil and grass rose up between it and Violet . . . and then stopped right before impact.

"I'm so, so sorry," the puppy said.

Violet looked around the park to see where else the voice could be coming from. "Who's there?" she asked. "Who's pretending to be a talking puppy?"

"It's me. I'm the one talking," it said as it began to pound its tail on the grass. The ground shook, and Violet struggled to keep her balance. The puppy continued, "Usually, I forget to say I'm sorry, but I remembered this time. Sorry!"

Violet was sure that the puppy's mouth was moving, but still couldn't quite believe that she was standing in front of a talking dog. Instinctively, she went to the one thing that always made sense, her to-do list. "Meet Godzilla puppy and try not to die," it reminded her. She put a check mark next to "try not to die" and moved on to the first part of that sentence, the meet-Godzilla part.

The puppy's chin was slightly above her head, so Violet stood on her tiptoes

to look into its large brown eyes. She said, "Hello, talking Godzilla puppy. My name is Violet."

The ground vibrated as the puppy thumped its tail like a jackhammer and responded, "I'm Moose, and you're the first human I've ever met, and it's the best thing ever! Hi-hi-hi-hi-hiya!" He followed up this introduction with a giant full-body lick that lifted Violet off her feet.

In ordinary circumstances, Violet would have made a list detailing all the ways she would disinfect, scrub, and sanitize herself, but there was something unusual about this lick. It left her covered in some kind of glittery, sparkly dust. She looked at Moose more closely and realized that his fur was sparkly, too. "That was too many *hi*'s and you left your puppy sparkles all over me," she said.

"I know! Isn't it great?" Moose grinned as he shook himself off and scattered more sparkles everywhere.

"Happens when I use my superpowers." He lifted his feet high and pranced around the park to show off. "'Cause I'm a superpuppy!" he said as he left large paw-shaped holes in the grass. "And I'm superstrong," he added, as though Violet couldn't already see what his strength had done to the park.

Violet bent down over her list, erased the nineteen and a half other things she'd planned to do that day, and wrote, "Learn all about superpuppies named Moose." She was about to begin a new list of all the things she needed to know about him when she noticed a commotion at the other side of the park. The concerned citizens had returned with a couple of concerned police officers. Violet made a quick decision and said, "C'mon, Moose. I need to get you out of here."

Violet and Moose heard someone shout, "It's over there!" They turned to see a woman pointing at them.

Violet turned to Moose. "And by *it*, they mean you. Let's go!" She considered adding "run away with Moose" to her list but decided it was better to run first and plan later. *This isn't like me at all*, she thought as she and Moose hurtled side by side out of the park.

CHAPTER THREE

The Cement River

Moose loved to run. He didn't know where he was going, but wherever it was, he was excited about it. There were so many new smells in this human world. The sidewalk gave off an odor from all the feet that had walked on it before him. He smelled sneakers from a gym, high heels from a party, loafers from an office, and sandals from a picnic. He would have kept his nose pressed to that sidewalk all day if something round and ball-shaped hadn't rolled right past him. *Magic ball!* he thought as a big metal thing with wheels—which Moose recognized from his human studies class as a car—drove between him and the ball.

He leaped off the sidewalk and ran after it. "Come back, magic ball!" he yelled. But his voice was drowned out by all the metal things zooming around him. Moose knew that Rocky would have known which one was a bus, which one was a motorcycle, and which one was a car, but he was too flustered to come up with a single word for any of them. As wheeled things continued to speed around him, he realized he was standing in the middle of a cement river, something humans called a road. He also remembered that he'd been warned to stay away from these things. Having no idea what to do next, Moose did what he always did when he was afraid. He dropped to his belly and put his paws over his eyes. "Oh noooooooo!" he howled.

Moose wasn't exactly sure what happened next. There was some kind of shrieking and blaring and honking. He heard humans yelling. They sounded concerned and worried and maybe a little angry. He lifted one paw from his eye and saw Violet, his new human and bestest friend forever, standing in the middle of the cement river. She was holding both of her hands over her head with her fingers spread out. She looked fearless as she stared down all the metal things that had stopped zooming around them. He didn't know what kind of magic she had, but he loved her for it. He jumped to his feet. "Thank you, thank you, thank you, magic car stopper!" he said as he bounded to her side.

Violet looked at him. Her eyebrows were closer together than they'd been before, and the corners of her mouth were pointing down. "We need to

go over some rules," she said. Moose nodded, but before he could tell her that he'd do absolutely anything for her, a person on a two-wheeled thing with no motor zipped between two of the stopped cars. It was headed right at them.

"Watch out for the bike!" Violet yelled as she grabbed him and scrambled to get them both out of the way.

Moose wasn't going to let anything happen to his amazing new friend. The bike needed to watch out for him. He jumped between Violet and the human on the bike and stood his ground. The bike hit him squarely and painlessly on the side. He heard the metal crumple and saw the human fly over his head.

"Whoaaa!" the human yelled as Moose ran to help soften the impact.

The human landed on Moose's soft back with a solid *thwamp* that sent sparkles flying into the air.

"What's happening?" a deep voice asked.

Moose rolled to his side so the human could get off and turned to sniff. He let his nose travel along the human's body. It was a male human who smelled like sweat and french fries and . . . an Earth dog?!? The idea of an Earth dog made Moose's tail wag uncontrollably.

It pounded into the crumpled bike, instantly smashing it into tiny pieces.

The man stared in shock at his destroyed bike, the giant dog, and the girl covered in sparkles. "For real, seriously, like, what's happening?" he asked again.

Other humans started to get out of their cars, and they were moving fast. Two male humans helped the man to his feet while a female human hugged Violet and asked her if she was okay. Moose would have found this human behavior very fascinating if he hadn't suddenly spotted the magic ball in the middle of the street.

Moose thundered across the street, cracking the pavement in his wake. He heard a few humans scream in surprise, but he didn't care. His mission was to retrieve that ball, and nothing was going to stop him! It was hard for Moose to be anything but strong, but he gently put his teeth around the ball and lifted it in his mouth. He was ready to carry it to Violet when something dropped over his neck. "I've got your dog, sweetie," a human behind him said. Moose heard a click and felt something on his neck tighten and pull him.

Moose whirled around and saw that the female human who had hugged Violet was holding a long cord that was attached to this thing around his neck. He immediately remembered *collar* and *leash* from his human studies. He knew there were rules about what to do if he was ever unlucky enough to be in this situation, but he couldn't remember any of them, so he ran.

The woman dropped the leash as Moose galloped to Violet, lowered his head, and flipped her onto his back. "Moose!" she yelled, but he didn't respond. The magic ball was still in his mouth, and he had to get it somewhere safe. Violet yelled, "Moose!" again, and when he didn't slow down, he felt her give in to the moment. She wrapped her legs around his chest and held on to

this new collar thing. He didn't mind her hands around his neck. It felt like they belonged there.

Moose carried Violet down an alley and then dropped to his belly so she could climb off. She stood in front of him with her hands on her hips and said, "There are soooo many rules you need to learn." She pulled a notepad and pen out of her pocket and began to write. "Rule number one: Humans don't ride dogs." She brushed magic sparkles off of her clothes and continued, "Rule number two: Dogs don't shed sparkly stuff all over the place."

Moose was pretty sure that neither of her rules were accurate. She was perfectly capable of riding him, and he most definitely shed magic sparkles every time he used his superstrength. He was also sure that unless he changed the subject, he was going to hear a lot more rules. He dropped the ball at her feet and thumped his tail. "I'm in your world to find this magic ball," he said as he nosed it in her direction. "And here it is," he added, thrilled to be doing so well on his mission.

Violet picked up the ball with two fingers and then held it as far away from her body as she could. "This doesn't look like a magic ball," she said. "It looks like a pine cone . . . a drool-covered pine cone," she added as she wiped her fingers on her jeans.

Moose's tail stopped wagging. "Is a pine cone bad?" he asked.

Violet shook her head. "Pine cones aren't good or bad. They grow on trees, and there are lots of them all over the place, especially the park."

Moose sniffed the pine cone. He smelled wood, pine, squirrels, and a little bit of that road where he'd found it. He hung his head in disappointment. "But I'm supposed to find the magic ball."

Out of the corner of his eye, Moose saw the corners of Violet's mouth finally curl up. "Don't worry. I can help." Moose's heart soared as she grabbed his leash to lead him home.

CHAPTER FOUR

No Takesie Backsies

It didn't take long for Violet to realize that no one wanted to share the sidewalk with a sparkle-covered girl and her giant dog. They were given so much space to walk that she and Moose could carry on a conversation without anyone else even noticing. And this was a good thing, because Violet had a lot to say. She'd finished sharing her list of "Moose rules," and Moose had nodded along, promising that he could follow every single one of them. But there was one rule that was so much more important than all the others, she had to repeat it. "What's the big rule, Moose?" she asked.

"I am not a horse," he answered confidently.

Violet shook her head and sighed. "Nope, the other big rule."

Moose thought for a moment, concentrating with all his might, and then, with slightly less confidence, said, "Don't squash the dads."

Violet was ready to sigh again but had to admit that was a pretty big rule, too. "Okay, there are *two* big rules. Don't squash either of the dads, especially not before they give me permission to have a puppy," she said. "And don't talk in front of my dads or any other person besides me."

Moose stopped walking. Violet tugged on the leash even though she already knew how pointless it was. She was no match for Moose's strength. "That seems like a bad rule. How'm I supposed to be friends with humans I can't talk to?" he asked.

This was a reasonable question, but Violet hated reasonable questions when they didn't go her way. She wasn't sure if she didn't want Moose to talk to her parents because they'd freak out or because she wanted to keep Moose and this amazing secret all to herself. Either way, she answered with "'Cause I said so." That was good enough for Moose. He shook it off and started to walk again.

As Violet climbed the stairs to the brownstone she lived in with her two dads, she tried to picture their reaction to her bringing home a giant puppy. But she didn't have to wonder about this for long because Pops and Daddy were waiting for her. They threw open the front door with their usual gusto. "We're so happy you're home . . ." There was probably more to that sentence, but Violet never heard it. The dads were too busy staring at her and Moose.

Daddy finally exhaled and said, "Sorry, I thought you were my daughter, Violet, but my Violet would *never* come home covered in dirt and grass."

Pops beamed and added, "Or sparkles. Our girl does not do sparkles, and believe me, I've tried."

Violet's dads grinned at each other.

They were enjoying this. Pops nudged his husband. "And you know what else our Violet would never do?"

Daddy finished, "Come home with a giant puppy!"

"So, tell us . . . who are you?" Pops asked her.

Violet waited until they were done. "Can I have a puppy?" she asked as she led Moose past them and through the front door like it was already decided.

Violet knew her dads were following her as she continued down the hallway and into the kitchen at the back of the house. "His name is Moose, and I've made a list of the things he needs: food, organic of course; a nice set of dishes, formal and everyday; an extra-extra-large bed; a new collar and leash, preferably purple; and a name tag that says 'Moose Belongs to Violet and Her Dads.'"

"Awww," the dads said at once, and Violet spun around, knowing that she was very close to getting what she wanted.

Pops and Daddy hugged Violet. "I knew my little list maker was somewhere under all that dirt," Pops said. Violet hugged them back. They really were the best dads ever.

"Oh yeah, he also needs a bath," she added.

"He's not the only one." Daddy laughed, and Violet had to agree. She

was a mess, but first things first. Violet moved aside so they could really see Moose in all his full, drooly, sparkly, happy glory.

"Pops and Daddy, this is Moose. Moose, this is Pops and Daddy. Welcome to the family!" she said.

Pops and Daddy dropped to their knees and began to pet Moose. "Who's a good boy?" they asked. Moose seemed to think he was the good boy and thumped his tail joyfully, cracking the tile floor. He then began a thunderous happy dance that splintered two kitchen chairs and wiped out a leg of the kitchen table. This caused the fruit bowl to slide off the table and land on Moose's back. He yelped so loudly that it sent Violet and the dads reeling backward. They slid across the linoleum on their butts while Moose tried to run away from the chaos he'd just created. He hit the kitchen rug with such force that it took off like a sled.

He slid across the kitchen and slammed into the back door, which flew off its hinges and landed in the backyard with a tremendous crash.

Moose lowered his head and tucked his tail between his legs as the dads stared at the wreckage in silence. They were speechless, but Violet was not.

"You said I could keep him. No takesie backsies!" she said.

Finally, Pops managed to speak. "Obedience school," he croaked. "Lots and lots of obedience school."

Violet jumped to her feet. "That's settled, then. C'mon, Moose, I wanna show you our bedroom." The dads stared as Moose dutifully got to his feet

and trotted to her side. "And get your sparkles out now so they don't end up all over the carpet upstairs," she said.

Moose got the sparkles out by shaking himself. It was a full-body shake that caused a cloud of drool, fur, and sparkles to form around the dads. As the mess rained down around them, Daddy turned to Pops. "So, which one of us gave her permission to have a puppy again?"

CHAPTER FIVE

Yell "Cat" Like a Man

Moose was stretched out on Violet's bed. He would have made room for her, but she was too busy staring at that thing he didn't like. It looked like a book, but it hummed and smelled like electricity, and kept Violet from doing what he wanted her to do, which was scratch his ears. He really, really liked having his ears scratched.

"Whatcha doing?" he asked.

Violet answered without looking at him. "I'm using my laptop to look for your magic ball. I mean, if there's a magic ball bouncing around the city somewhere, somebody's definitely going to post about it." Moose had no idea what she was talking about and yawned loudly to show her just how much he didn't care about this laptop thing.

"Wanna give me a treat?" he asked.

Violet shook her head. "You've had, like, ten million already, along with Pop's pasta, Daddy's salad, and my dessert." Moose licked his chops, remembering how much he liked human food.

Moose sat up and stared at the back of Violet's head. "Wanna scratch my ears?" he asked hopefully. Now that he'd had a little bit of that human affection he'd heard so much about, he wanted more, so much more.

Violet finally turned around and looked at him. "I wanna help you be super. I mean, if you're a superpuppy here to be super, then we should be the best girl-and-her-dog superhero team ever!"

Moose's mouth opened, and his tongue dropped from his mouth. This was his version of a grin, and he was grinning because he was happy. *Girl and her dog* . . . He'd never heard words that he liked as much as those. She was his girl, and he was her dog. What could be better than that?! And as if she could read his mind, Violet reached over and scratched his ears. His girl scratching her dog's ears was, *actually*, the best thing ever!

"I just don't understand why you didn't get any more instructions besides 'find the magic ball.' I mean, if I was going to send a superdog on a supermission, I would have at least made a list of all the things that that superdog was supposed to do," Violet mused.

"CAT!" Moose yelled so suddenly that Violet fell off her chair. Seconds later, Shadow appeared on Violet's desk. "Hi, Shadow," Moose said, happy to see his friend. "You gotta meet the bestest human who ever lived."

Shadow briefly turned her golden eyes on Violet and then disappeared as quickly as she'd come. The dads threw open the bedroom door and barreled in. "Did someone just yell 'cat'? Did a loud man yell 'cat'?" Pops asked.

Daddy looked wildly around the room and then let his eyes settle on Violet. "Did you just yell 'cat' like a man?" he asked.

Violet crawled up onto her chair and shook her head. "I just said 'AHH' 'cause I fell off my chair," she said, and then continued, "Why would I yell 'cat'? It's not like a big gray one just appeared out of nowhere or anything."

The dads looked at each other. "No, of course not. That would be weird," Pops said.

"Guess we're all tired. It's been a big day. Lights out, please," Daddy said as he went to kiss Violet good night.

Moose sat up expectantly. "Me?"

he asked, and then realized he'd just broken Violet's big rule . . . again. Pops and Daddy stopped in their tracks for a surprised moment and then grinned.

Pops threw his arms around Moose and kissed his head. "Isn't that cute? It sounded just like Moose was asking for a good night kiss, too." He looked down at his sparkle-covered shirt. "This really is the strangest thing ever."

Daddy rubbed Moose's head, and Moose thought his heart might burst. He loved his new humans and wanted Sparkle, Rocky, and Tobey to meet them, too, and his parents would love them so much . . . Suddenly, the happiness drained out of Moose's body as he remembered his parents and the other big dogs. They were still missing, and it was his job to figure out what happened to them. What was he doing enjoying human hugs and kisses?!

The minute the dads closed the door, Shadow reappeared. She seemed to be having the same thought as Moose. "What are you doing about finding the magic ball?" Shadow asked.

Moose was about to tell her about the pine cone when Violet leaped to his defense. "Moose and I were just making a plan. At the top of the list is . . ."

The briefest of purrs escaped from Shadow's throat. "I love lists," she said. Violet's face lit up, and Moose let out a low growl. He didn't like the way they liked each other. Shadow lifted her paw and launched a stream of magic at his hindquarters. He felt the zap and was ready to object loudly, when he remembered what happened the last time he made too much noise.

"Mind your manners," Shadow hissed.

Moose glowered at Shadow. "We have a plan," he lied.

"Mmmm-hmmm," Shadow replied, clearly not believing him. "What is it, then?" she asked.

"I was just googling 'magic ball,'" Violet told her, "but I didn't find anything."

Shadow turned to the annoying

laptop thing like she understood why anyone would bother looking at it in the first place. "Show me," she said.

Violet hit some little square things below the laptop, and it lit up. Moose saw a bunch of pictures of human things on it. "I've been looking to see if anyone's posted about a magic ball."

Shadow leaned in close to look at the screen and then used her paw to point to a picture. "What's that?" she asked. Violet made the picture bigger, and there it was. Moose could see it, too. There was a picture of a sparkly, undoubtedly magic ball sitting on a platform in a big room with lots of arches.

Violet was excited. "The ball is an exhibit at the museum," she said. "It says they're showing a mystery ball to the public. No one knows what it is!" She turned to Moose and Shadow and grinned. "Except us. We know exactly what it is and what we have to do, don't we, team?"

Moose nodded and said, "We have to go to this museum place and get our ball!"

Violet considered this. "Yes we do, buuut . . . you can't just walk into a museum and take things, so we're going to have to make a plan, and that means . . ."

"A new list!" Violet and Shadow said at once.

CHAPTER SIX

Sweet Lovie Fuzz Muffin

"I don't think that's a good idea, Vee," Daddy said.

"Dogs probably aren't even allowed in the museum . . . especially ones who haven't been to obedience school," Pops added, mentioning obedience school for the umpteenth time since Violet had brought Moose home.

Violet was prepared for this. She threw her arms around Moose's neck and hugged him tightly. "Remember what I showed you," she whispered. Moose remembered. He hung his head and let out a long, heartbreaking whine while Violet fake cried into his fur. The dads were unimpressed.

"And the Oscar for best fake cry goes to Violet and Moose!" Daddy said as he and Pops clapped.

Violet lifted her tear-free face and grimaced. "Fine," she said. "We can leave Moose here by himself." She let that sink in for a moment and then added, "He probably won't even break anything."

Pops and Daddy moved like

lightning. Pops snatched the leash from the counter as Daddy grabbed his backpack full of snacks. "Well done, Violet. Well done," Daddy said as they headed for the front door.

As they started down the stairs to the sidewalk, Violet pulled out her list and checked off step number one: "Get the dads to agree to take me and Moose to the museum." Her eyes moved down to step number two: "Take a taxi to the museum."

Pops was already on it. "Taxi," he yelled. A taxi slowed down just long enough for the driver to see Moose, and then sped away.

"Taxi, taxi, taxi!" Pops and Daddy

yelled at every yellow cab that passed by, but no one stopped.

"TAXI!" Moose bellowed so loudly that the ground shook. Brakes squealed as every car, taxi or not, screeched to a halt. Pops and Daddy looked around, wondering where the voice came from and how it could possibly be that loud.

"What was that?!" Pops asked, slightly stunned.

Horns began to honk, and Violet made a decision. "We should take the bus today," she said as she tugged on Moose's leash and headed for the bus stop.

The dads followed and were still wondering where that voice came from when a bus pulled up and the doors opened. Violet walked up the stairs and tugged lightly on the leash. "C'mon, Moose. Time for your first bus ride," she said. But Moose wasn't coming. He wedged his front paws into the first step of the bus and anchored his butt on the sidewalk. He shook his head, silently letting her know that he was NOT getting on that bus. "C'mon, Moose. There's nothing to be afraid of. It's just a bus, and it's gonna take us to the museum. Remember? It's all part of the plan," Violet said.

Violet wished she could ask Moose if he was still nervous about the time he chased the pine cone into the road, but she didn't want him to answer. He'd already said a few too many words in front of the dads, and a full sentence about what he was and wasn't afraid of would definitely give him away as a talking superpuppy.

Pops and Daddy pushed on Moose's hindquarters. Sparkles floated like clouds around his body, but he didn't budge.

"Get a move on, Moose! The bus can't go anywhere until you get on or off," Daddy said.

Behind him, Pops waved apologetically. "Sorry about the dog . . . and the sparkles," he said to the driver, who smiled back like this was the best thing she'd seen in a while.

Somewhere farther down the aisle of the bus, a dog barked, and Moose immediately perked up. He leaned forward so that he could peer into the bus. Violet followed his gaze to another girl about her age sitting with a small, weirdly dressed little dog on her lap. On the seat next to her, there was a serious-looking, beautiful gray dog with long legs, a pointy nose, and an ornate rhinestone collar.

"Rocky!" Moose yelled as he leaped into the bus and thundered down the aisle. The bus shook with every step. Confused passengers screamed and held on, but Moose didn't stop until he reached this other girl and her dog.

Moose's tail wagged so hard that the bus began to rock back and forth like a ship on rough water. Violet staggered down the aisle, trying to get to him. She was almost there when she heard the gray dog growl softly at Moose, "Not okay, Moose! Dogs don't talk here." Violet barely had time to process the fact that there was another talking dog in the world before the girl leaped from her seat.

"Out the back way, Sweet Lovie Fuzz," the girl said as she pulled the cord

to open the back door of the bus. Violet stared in shock as the gray dog ignored the door and simply leaped through the side of the bus.

The dog landed so gracefully that it was hard to imagine that it had just jumped through metal and glass. Violet never would have believed it if she

hadn't happened to have a superdog of her own. Moose galloped down the stairs after them. "Wait!" Violet said as she followed. The moment her feet touched the pavement, the bus pulled away. Violet looked up just in time to see Pops and Daddy press their faces to the glass as the bus carried them down the street.

Violet held up a finger in the girl's direction and said, "Don't go anywhere, new girl. I just have to text my dads and tell them to meet me at the museum."

Moose jumped on the gray dog, which tried to remain stoic for a beat and then clearly couldn't help himself. They wrestled and played. Moose body-

slammed a mailbox that fell on top of and right through the other dog. "Aren't they the best things ever? That's my magic dog, Sweet Lovie Fuzz Muffin," the new girl said.

Moose suddenly stopped playing and stared at the girl and then the dog and then back at the girl and then directly at the sleek gray dog. "Sweet Lovie Fuzz Muffin?!" he asked, and then laughed so loud and so hard that the new girl and the little dog in her arms were thrown backward onto the sidewalk.

The gray dog was at the girl's side in an instant. "Are you all right?" he asked.

She nodded cheerfully, jumped to her feet, and threw one arm around

Violet while holding the little dog in the other. Violet stiffened as the girl said, "I'm Nova, and we're like sisters 'cause we both have magic puppies. If you don't need all your wishes, can I have them?"

Violet closed her eyes and waited until the hug was over. When the girl was done, Violet stuck out her hand the way she'd seen adults greet each other. "I'm Violet, and I'm pretty sure we have *super*puppies that don't grant wishes."

Nova looked sad for a moment and then nodded in agreement. "Super-duper, best ever *magic* puppies!"

The gray dog said, "I'm Rocky,

Moose's brother. We're here to find four magic balls and save our parents."

"Different balls, same parents!" Moose added.

Violet's phone rang. She didn't have to answer it to know that there were two frantic dads on the other end. "Good luck finding your ball!" she said as she grabbed Moose's leash and ran toward the museum.

✧ CHAPTER SEVEN ✧

Humans with Hats

Moose couldn't stop thinking about his brother and the girl who smelled like bubble gum and roses and called Rocky "Sweet Lovie Fuzz Muffin." He couldn't wait to tell Tobey and Sparkle about Rocky's name change, even though thinking about his family was confusing. For the first time in his life, he didn't know where they were or what they were doing, and he missed them. He just hoped they were as lucky as he and Rocky were and had humans of their own to give them attention and snacks and help them find their own magic balls. He smiled gratefully at his human, who was still breathing hard from their race to the museum.

"There it is," she gasped as she pointed to a big building in front of them. Moose could see Pops and Daddy waiting for them on a wide staircase.

Pops and Daddy were happy to see them and had lots of hugs and pets for both of them. Moose wasn't sure what he did to be such a good boy until Violet asked them, "Why're you guys so happy? I thought you'd be mad we got separated."

Pops moved to scratch Moose's ears, but Moose had a better idea. He turned around so that Pops's hand was over his favorite spot above his tail. "Turns out when your little girl is with a weirdly strong, enormous, sparkly puppy, there's a lot less to worry about." Moose wagged his tail with pride. It slammed into Pops's side and knocked him over. He rolled down the stairs with an "AHHHH" and landed on the sidewalk below.

"Owwww," Pops whined as he looked at his torn pants and scraped elbow. Moose tucked his tail between his legs. That was probably his fault.

Daddy dashed down the stairs and helped Pops to his feet. "Just a scratch, a few bruises. You'll be okay, but I hate to break it to you . . . Your pants aren't gonna make it," he said with a fake sob.

Violet whispered in Moose's ear, "Daddy's a doctor, so Pops should listen to him, but he won't. He likes to diagnose himself." Moose nodded like he understood what she was talking about. He had a lot of questions but knew this wasn't the time to ask any of them.

Pops limped up the stairs and claimed, "Something is definitely broken this time." Daddy sighed and told him that once he washed up, he'd be fine.

Violet and Moose followed Pops and Daddy to the big door where a man with a funny thing on his head pointed at Moose. "Sorry, no dogs in the museum."

Moose let out a long, low growl. He wasn't about to let this human get between him and the magic ball.

The man backed away but didn't change his mind. "Dogs aren't allowed."

"I just need to use the men's room, and then we'll find something else fun to do today," Pops said, more to Violet than the man. Moose felt Violet bristle beside him and understood that she wasn't going to let this human get between her and that magic ball, either.

"You guys go in. We'll wait for you out here," Violet said, but she wasn't telling the truth. Almost before they were through the door, she was pulling Moose toward the back of the building. It wasn't as crowded as the entrance, but the humans behind the building were moving much faster. They went in and out, and Moose saw that some of them had the same funny things on their heads as the man out front.

Moose hid behind a dumpster so he could finally ask Violet those questions.

"What're we gonna do next, and who was that man with that funny thing on his head, and what was that funny thing, and why do some of those other humans have the same funny things on their heads?" he asked all at once.

Violet answered, "The man who wouldn't let you in was a security guard, and that thing on his head is called a hat. And when we get inside, there are going to be a lot more people with the same kind of hats trying to kick you out of the museum, so you have to stay away from all of them."

"Or, if they get in my way, I can knock them over," Moose said.

"That's not a good idea," Shadow

said, seconds before she appeared on top of the dumpster.

"Cat!" Moose yelled, a little late, but still loud. Moose peeked around the edge of the dumpster to see if anyone else heard him, but the humans were still pulling things out of a big vehicle. They didn't seem to notice.

Shadow gave another one of those long, slow cat blinks and continued, "Try not to knock any humans over. This is a peaceful mission."

"That's right. Superheroes only knock over the bad guys," Violet said, and then added, "Security guards are just annoying."

"How are we gonna get past those annoying security guards if we don't knock them over?" Moose wanted to know.

"I suggest the loading dock, where they're taking art into the museum. Pretend you're a masterpiece, and I'll see you in there," Shadow said, just before disappearing.

"Brilliant," Violet whispered as she readjusted something on her list. Moose felt that sensation again, the one that made him want to growl at Shadow even though she'd already disappeared. He needed to have some brilliant ideas of his own.

"I'm brilliant, too!" he said as he galloped toward the humans in their hats.

He heard Violet gasp behind him.

"Wait, Moose! That's not part of the plan!" But it was too late. The humans had seen him, and they were staring. He was getting closer but had no idea what he'd do once he got to them.

"That's a big dog," one of the humans said.

"Real big . . . and is it covered in sparkles?" asked another.

Moose was almost on them. His footsteps were shaking the vehicle, which was bouncing on its wheels. Moose stepped down hard. The pavement split under his paws, and the cracks spread all the way to the humans' feet. They were frozen in place.

And then that moment was gone. The humans ran, and in a matter of seconds, the place was completely people-free. Moose slowed down and let Violet catch up to him. "You're right, Moose. That was pretty brilliant," she panted. Moose felt something in his chest expand. He was working himself up for a happy dance but stopped when Violet gestured to some of the large wooden boxes the humans had left behind. "Those crates are probably full of art that's going into the museum. We should pretend we're masterpieces, remember?" She tapped her list and continued with a frown, "It was kind of part of the plan, but I'm still putting it on the list like it was always there."

Violet adjusted her list and then walked up to one of the big boxes and ran her hands across it. "Do you think there's a handle here or something?" she asked.

Moose didn't bother to look. He used his paw to hit the side of the wooden box. A panel fell out, leaving just enough room for them to crawl in. Now all they had to do was wait.

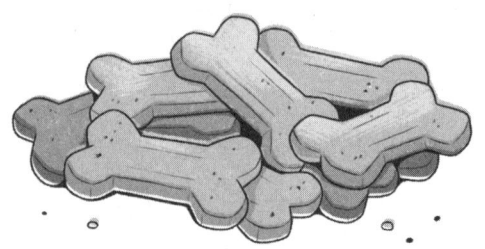

Treat Breath

Violet was beginning to regret giving Moose so many snacks, because the crate was quickly filling up with his treat breath. A statue of something that looked like an angry fairy was poking her in the back, and she couldn't reach her phone, which was vibrating with all the fury of two dads who were expecting an answer.

Violet was ready for the workers to come back already, and then when Moose's ears perked up, she knew they were finally on their way. After a moment, she heard a man ask, "You ever seen a dog like that?"

"Wish I got a video of that glittery behemoth," a woman said.

Moose nudged her, and Violet knew he wanted to know what a behemoth was. "Big," she whispered as they heard a dolly slide under the crate. The crate suddenly went sideways as one of the people outside started to wheel them somewhere. Violet felt the air get cooler and hoped that meant they'd made it inside. She wanted to put a big check mark next to "get inside with Moose" and wished she'd thought of it before she climbed in the box and sat on her list.

Violet heard the workers walk away, and she kicked the panel loose. She poked her head out and looked around. She was happy to see they were inside the building and alone. "C'mon, Moose," she said as she climbed out. They were in a big warehouse-type space with lots of crates that looked like the one they'd just crawled out of. At one end, she could see daylight, and at the other was a door that she hoped led into the museum.

Her phone vibrated again, and she quickly texted the dads. **I'm in the museum. Find me**, she wrote. She knew that wasn't enough information to keep them happy, but it would keep them busy while she and Moose searched for the magic ball.

Violet pushed the door open and walked into a dark room where people

were watching a video about a girl with green hair who made pots from trash. The green-haired girl kept everyone interested enough that Moose and Violet could cross the room to another door. They stepped into a large room filled with exhibits of all kinds. She saw marble statues of women and angels, busts of serious-looking men, pots that looked suspiciously like trash, and a huge *T. rex* skeleton that loomed over everything, but she didn't see a magic ball anywhere.

"Maybe it's behind all those humans," Moose whispered. Violet looked in the direction his nose was pointing and agreed that he was probably right.

Everyone in the room seemed to be fixated on one particular exhibit. Violet motioned for Moose to follow as they joined the crowd.

Violet stood on her tiptoes but couldn't see past the adults. She tried to wriggle through their legs, but it was too tight. "We need to find out if that's the magic ball," she said.

Moose nodded and lowered himself to the ground. "Get on," he said. Violet climbed onto his back, and he stood up on his hind legs. Violet was suddenly much taller than everyone around her and had a perfect view of the magic ball. It was on a pedestal that was surrounded by ropes to keep people

back, even though no one looked particularly interested in getting close to it. The ball was pulsating, changing colors, and randomly spitting out sparks of magic.

"That's right, folks," someone from the museum said. "This is the museum's newest piece. No one knows what it is or why it's so colorful and sparkly, but as far as we know, this museum is the only place you'll ever see one." The crowd murmured as Moose lowered Violet back down to the floor.

"Definitely the magic ball," Violet said, "but I don't know how we're supposed to get it."

"I'd suggest a distraction," Shadow said, right before she appeared on the head of a bust.

Violet grabbed Moose's snout and held it shut. "Don't do it. Don't yell 'cat!' " she insisted.

Moose whimpered, and Violet let go. *"Caaaaat!"* he whispered.

Shadow wrapped her tail around the chin of the bust and continued, "You need to find a way to get all those humans away from the ball."

Violet looked at the backs of all the people gathered around the ball and felt frustration welling up inside her. "But this wasn't on the list," she said.

"All these people around the magic ball were NOT part of my plan!"

Shadow flicked her tail and disappeared. Violet turned to Moose in surprise and said, "She left! Shadow just left us!"

Moose nodded. "She used to do that to me and my brother and sisters all the time. Usually when she wanted us to learn something."

Violet let that sink in but didn't like where it was leading. She responded reluctantly, "Like, maybe I don't always need to have a plan?"

Moose gave her a full-body lick that lifted her off her feet and left her covered in sparkles. When she was back on the floor, she said, "Still gross . . . but you know what? I'll wait until I'm home to make a list of all the things I need to clean." She spoke to the air. "Take that, Shadow!"

Moose thumped his tail on the floor. The vibration knocked the bust off of its pedestal. As it crashed to the floor, everyone in the room turned around to look. There was a collective gasp of shock as they took in the girl, her giant dog, and the broken bust.

"Guess that takes care of the distraction part," Violet said, and then gestured toward the room. "You do something to get them away from the ball, and I'll . . . I'll just grab it, I guess."

"Good idea!" Moose said as he thundered into the crowd. People yelled as they ran for cover. Somewhere a guard reminded anyone who would listen that dogs weren't allowed in the museum, but Violet only had one thing on her mind. She needed to grab that magic ball!

Violet followed Moose toward the ball. She could see it there in front of her. She had one foot over the rope divider when a woman accidentally slammed into her. "Sorry, but there's a giant dog on the loose!" she said as she scurried away.

Violet saw Moose spin in her direction. "Violet! Are you okay?" he shouted. His voice echoed through the nearly empty space.

And then, from the other side of the room, she heard her name again. "Violet! Violet!" She turned to see the dads frantically running toward her.

Violet knew she had to act fast, or they'd never get that ball. She turned to Moose and yelled, "Forget all the rules, Moose! Especially that one about how dogs are not for riding."

Moose didn't hesitate. He lowered

his head and lifted her onto his back. She wrapped her legs around his chest and threw her arms around his neck. "Now get that ball," she said as Moose galloped toward the exhibit.

CHAPTER NINE

Bones and Bad Guys

Violet's weight on his back felt just right. She was close and safe, and Moose was finally going to wrap his teeth around that magic ball. He was only a few steps from the pedestal where the ball sat when an unusually thin man wearing dark clothes and a hood that hid his face stepped gracefully over the ropes and plucked the ball from its pedestal.

"That's mine!" Moose bellowed, not caring who heard him. "Give it back!"

Moose jumped, launching himself at the man, but the man was quick and agile. He pivoted so fast that when Moose landed, the man was already behind them.

"Hey! That guy has our ball!" Violet yelled as Moose caught a whiff of him. He smelled sharp and metallic, like a combination of fire, earth, and magic, and Moose knew he wasn't just any guy. He was someone from a magic world, and he wasn't friendly.

Moose let out a long, low growl, and the man hesitated. Moose suddenly

smelled salt and sweat and realized that whoever or whatever this was, it still wasn't sure about facing off against a giant puppy with superstrength. The man spun toward the door. The only thing between him and the exit was Pops and Daddy, and they were coming fast. Moose heard them say things like "young lady," "unacceptable," "grounded," and "no screen time," but he didn't have time to figure out what it all meant. Instead, he was wondering what this magic man would do to humans who were in his way.

Violet yelled, "That's a bad guy! Stop him."

Pops and Daddy slowed down. They seemed confused by what they were seeing. "Violet, are you *riding* Moose?!" Pops asked as Daddy focused on the man. Daddy tensed up, and Moose knew that Daddy felt what he already knew. This strange man was trouble.

"What's going on here?" Daddy asked in a voice more serious than Moose had heard before. In response, the man wriggled his fingers and swung his arm. A stream of magic shot toward them. Pops yelped and pushed Daddy out of the way. The magic missed them both and instead sliced through the femur of the *T. rex* exhibit. Sparks rained down,

and the dinosaur skeleton began to rock back and forth. It was about to fall on the dads.

"Noooooo!" Moose yelled as he dropped his weight onto his haunches and then kicked off with all of his superpuppy strength. Violet was still clinging to his collar as he flew through the air, over the heads of Pops, Daddy, and the strange man.

Moose hit the *T. rex* skeleton like a bowling ball smashing into pins. The bones skittered across the room far away from Pops and Daddy. Moose landed with a floor-shattering thud and faced the man. "You're going to give me that ball!" he growled.

"Moose is talking! Moose is talking!" Pops shouted, and then nudged Daddy. "I told you Violet didn't yell 'cat' like a man," he added.

"My fault, I'm afraid," Shadow said as she appeared on top of a glass case containing a teacup display. Moose saw Pops's and Daddy's mouths move, but there was no sound coming out of them. He hoped they were all right.

The strange man stepped over the bones to get to the exit, and Moose whirled around to stop him. Violet fell sideways, barely managing to stay on his back. "Careful! Don't fall," Moose told her.

"Not a chance," Violet said as she pulled herself back up onto Moose's back. "I just needed to get this!" Moose turned his head to see what she was talking about. She held up one of the *T. rex* bones and grinned at him. "Now let's get that ball!"

Moose thundered toward the man while Violet brandished the dinosaur bone like a lance. The man turned back just long enough to shoot a stream of magic in their direction. Moose got down low and slid under the magic and across the room. As they skidded past the man, Violet swung the dinosaur bone and connected with the sparkly ball. It sailed across the room away from the exit.

"Catch it!" she yelled.

Moose watched as Daddy leaped to his feet and yelled, "Hut!" He ran across the room and let the ball fall into his outstretched hands.

"And here I just thought you were pretty," Pops told Daddy as he scrambled to his feet and grabbed a dinosaur bone of his own. He held it out in front of him, turned to the strange man, and said, "But my husband's not the only athlete in the family." Pops tapped the bone on the floor and then held it behind his shoulder with two hands. "You're looking at a softball state champ, two years in a row. Bring it on!" he said.

Moose had no idea what Pops was talking about, but he could see the strange man moving his fingers and knew what was coming next. "Magic!" Moose bellowed as the man sent another stream toward the dads. "Watch out!" Moose yelled again with such volume that the building shook, but he didn't have to warn them. Pops was ready. He took a step back and swung the bone right at the magic. It connected with a hiss, and little snakes of magic dropped to the floor and slithered harmlessly away.

"Keep whatever that was away from my family!" Pops bellowed.

Moose saw the strange man working the fingers of both hands and knew there was more magic coming, and he wasn't about to let any of it hit his humans. Moose lunged at the man, who ducked and spun on a spindly ankle, but before he could get away, Moose bit down on his hood and held on.

The strange man struggled, and the hood fell from his face. Moose stared at the moss-colored face with indigo eyes and knew for sure that this was not an Earth human.

"Give me the ball!" the nonhuman hissed in a voice that sounded like the howl of a windstorm. Suddenly, a stream of magic hit him in the arm. He hissed again as Moose turned to see Shadow on top of a display case. She pulled back her paw, ready to fire once more, when the man filled the room with a windy shriek so powerful that Violet had to bury her face in Moose's fur, while the dads dropped to their knees and covered their ears.

And then just as quickly as it started, the noise was gone and so was the man. All that was left were some burnt magic shards and his hood, still clamped in Moose's jaw.

Shadow smiled at Moose and said, "Well done, Moose. I hope your brother and sisters are as successful. I'll let you know . . ." And then she was gone.

Daddy helped Pops to his feet and asked, "What just happened?"

Moose felt Violet slide off of his back and drop to the floor beside him. "We're superheroes now," she said as she threw her arms around Moose's neck for a hug.

"And we just saved the day!" Moose said as he lifted Violet off her feet with another grateful, slobbery lick.

CHAPTER TEN

Superheroes

When Violet's feet were back on the floor, she saw the dads flinch. "It's okay, Vee. We've got some wet wipes around here somewhere..." Daddy trailed off as he looked around helplessly. "Wherever my backpack is."

Violet waved him off and said, "Don't need 'em. A little dog slobber never hurt anybody."

Pops looked startled but quickly recovered. "Good plan. Superheroes shouldn't be afraid of a little dog drool," he said.

"And I'm not so sure I need to have sooo many plans." She smiled lightly, teasing her dads. "I kind of like just letting things happen. It might be time to retire the list."

The dads gasped dramatically as Pops exchanged a look with his husband. "Dare to dream," he said.

Daddy frowned as something caught his attention. "Uh-oh," he said.

Violet followed his gaze to the other side of the room, where several museum guards were cautiously creeping out of their hiding places. "Humans with hats!" Moose said proudly as he thumped his tail on the floor.

"What happened here?" one of the guards asked.

The dads stared at each other hopelessly, not quite sure how to explain, but Violet was still feeling pretty super. "Earthquake," she said matter-of-factly.

"Are you sure?" another guard asked.

Violet used her elbow to poke Moose in the ribs. "Make me right," she whispered, and Moose obliged. He barked with all the force of a superpower puppy. The room shook as each bark ricocheted around the cavernous space, and the guards quickly scurried back to their hiding places.

"What do we do now?" Pops asked as he watched them retreat.

Daddy threw the magic ball up in the air and caught it again. "I say we take our magic ball and run!"

Violet laughed as she grabbed Moose's collar and pulled herself onto his back. "Who needs obedience school now?" she asked as they all ran laughing from the building.